STORM
ON THE
SEA

Text by Salima Alikhan

Raintree is an imprint of Capstone Global Library Limited, a company incorporated in England and Wales having its registered office at 264 Banbury Road, Oxford, OX2 7DY – Registered company number: 6695582

www.raintree.co.uk
myorders@raintree.co.uk

Original illustrations © Capstone Global Library Limited 2022
Originated by Capstone Global Library Ltd
Printed and bound in India

978 1 3982 1480 4

British Library Cataloguing in Publication Data
A full catalogue record for this book is available from the British Library.

Acknowledgements
We would like to thank the following for permission to reproduce photographs: Shutterstock/Monkik, 71

CONTENTS

CHAPTER 1

TRYING TO FORGET

"You can turn off the motor now!" Dad calls from the dock.

Aisha turns and looks past the side of her family's little sailing boat. The boat still doesn't have a name. Her mum and dad are standing there on the dock.

"OK!" she shouts back as she turns off the small outboard motor. She's hoisted the sails already. Now she's just sitting by the tiller, using it to steer around the small harbour.

Aisha's parents won't let her go out into the bay by herself. *At least they trust me to go this far*, Aisha thinks to herself.

They're letting her try out the boat in the harbour. She can go across the narrow inlet to the other side, where she can still see her parents perfectly.

It's the first time they've let her go out alone, and she doesn't want them to make her cut it short. She turns from them and tries to pretend they're not watching anxiously from the dock.

Aisha pretends she's all alone in the middle of a magic sea, sailing far away. The wind catches the sails and guides the little boat around. It's an amazing feeling.

The sailing boat has been quiet and patient all day, like she's been waiting for someone to get in. The boat feels like the only friend Aisha has these days.

It's almost sunset. Aisha looks out over the water. There's the marina and the other boats docked at the harbour.

"Aisha!" Mum calls. "Come back now!"

Aisha pretends not to hear and stays on the water.

Aisha's family comes to this bay every summer to relax. They like to swim, sail and barbecue.

But this year, it's different. It's the first year without Aisha's sister, Bianca. And without Bianca, it barely feels like the same place.

When Aisha looks at the dock, she remembers racing through it with Bianca, naming all the boats. Bianca was only a year older than Aisha – thirteen – and everyone always thought they were twins.

The only time Aisha can truly forget about what happened is when she's out on the water. On the water, she feels free. And she doesn't have to think about it.

"Dinnertime, Aisha! Come back now, young lady!" Dad calls.

She rolls her eyes.

Aisha really doesn't want to go back to her family's rental house. She's been doing everything she can to stay away from it.

But she obediently starts up the motor. She guides the boat back to the dock, making sure the fenders of the boat are out. Otherwise it would bump into the dock. She also makes sure the dock line is ready and tied to the boat.

She throws the other end of it to Dad, who grabs it and pulls the boat the rest of the way in. He ties it to the cleat, one of the metal posts on the dock where boats are tied, and Aisha clambers out of the boat.

"Good job," he says as he pats her on the back. "But next time, you come as soon as we call you."

"OK," Aisha agrees reluctantly.

"Burgers for dinner," Mum adds.

Aisha's stomach tightens. Burgers were Bianca's favourite. Has Mum forgotten that? Or has she finally stopped worrying about it?

Aisha drags her feet as she walks behind her parents and follows them back to the house.

CHAPTER 2

DON'T WANT TO TALK ABOUT IT

The three climb the crooked stone steps back to the family's rental house, which overlooks the harbour. The bay looks magical in the setting sun.

Aisha's younger brother, Sai, is waiting for them inside. He's bent over a puzzle on the coffee table with a very serious expression on his face. Sai is always very serious. Bianca was the only one who could really make him laugh.

"We're having burgers tonight," Dad tells Aisha again. He wants her to be excited. "Your favourite!"

"And I got some sparkling cider," Mum adds.

Aisha starts to get an itch she feels when she's trapped inside with her family. She gets it a lot these days. She doesn't like the way everyone pretends everything is OK, and no one will talk about Bianca.

Dad starts frying the burger patties. Aisha helps Mum set the table. Sai gets out the water and starts filling everyone's glass.

"Aisha just went out by herself for the first time," Mum tells Sai. "She did great."

"I think Bianca would have been proud of me," Aisha blurts out.

No one says anything at first.

"I think she would have," Mum says quietly.

Aisha's encouraged by this. A bunch of words she's been holding back come pouring out.

"I was thinking," Aisha says, "that when I was out there, it was almost like she was with me. Do you guys ever feel like that? Like she's still here?"

There's more silence. Sai gives Aisha a dark look, but she ignores him. Mum puts down her napkin and sips at her water, her face pale. Dad's hand shakes over the pan. Aisha waits in silence for a couple of moments before trying again.

"Don't you ever wonder if she can see us somehow?" Aisha asks. "I can't be the only one who wonders that. Where do you think she went?"

Now Mum's hand holding her glass shakes too. "I don't feel like thinking about that right now, Aisha."

"We don't need to talk about this at dinner," Dad says, as he puts burgers onto all the plates.

"Why not?" Aisha shouts. "Why can't we talk about it? Bianca would want us to talk about it! She wouldn't want us to just pretend it didn't happen!"

Everyone stares at her. Even Aisha wonders what's got into herself. She's usually pretty quiet. But she can't stand that her parents won't ever talk about Bianca.

To Aisha, they act like they want to pretend she didn't exist. *But Bianca did exist,* Aisha thinks fiercely. *She was my best friend in the world.*

"I'm not going to pretend she never existed! She might be dead now, but she was here!" Aisha throws down her napkin and storms to her room.

Her bedroom door is rickety, so when she slams it, the door doesn't make a very satisfying noise. She falls down on her bed and cries quietly.

Aisha hears her dad yell, "Come back out here and finish your food, Aisha. Right now."

She ignores him. She doesn't like being in this house, where they aren't even allowed to remember Bianca.

CHAPTER 3

SNEAKING AWAY

It's the middle of the night. Aisha's as quiet as a mouse as she tiptoes over the floor. Her boat shoes are in her hand. She doesn't want her family to hear her.

She slips as quietly as she can out the door and hurries to the docks. She loves the docks at night, and she's glad no one seems to be out right now. It's just her, the water, the boats and the moon.

Aisha makes her way towards the boat. She can't wait to get back on the water! It was the only time all day that she managed to forget about how weird her family was being.

She is sure Bianca would want her to do this. Bianca loved adventures. Most of all, she loved the water.

The boat looks like it's patiently waiting for Aisha. It's a small boat, a Catalina 22, which means it's only twenty-two feet long. But the family loves it.

Aisha steps inside, pulls on her life jacket, unties the dock line, and starts up the motor. She thinks it's about halfway full of fuel, which means it'll last about two hours. That's more than enough time. She just needs a few minutes alone on the water.

Aisha puts her hand on the tiller and looks at the harbour. She can see the rental house, dark and still. Just the idea of getting further away from it makes her feel better.

She hears a noise and whirls around.

It's Sai, standing on the dock, wearing pyjamas. He looks furious.

"What are you doing?" He's half-whispering. "You know you're not supposed to take the boat without telling anyone!"

"Mind your own business," Aisha says. "I just need a few minutes. I'll be right back."

"Get back here," he says.

Aisha frowns at him. He's acting like he's the boss of her even though she's a year older. "Make me," she says and turns on the motor.

Sai's eyes get huge. And then, suddenly he leaps into the water!

Aisha is so surprised she rushes over to the side of the boat to watch him. She can't believe it as he swims over to her.

"What are you doing?" Aisha asks. She doesn't have a choice but to let him crawl up onto the boat.

"We need to go back to the house," he pants.

Aisha shakes her head. "I just want to take it out for a few minutes. I can't stand being trapped in there with Mum and Dad. Please. Being out here makes it easier when I think about – about her."

Sai's face gets serious, but he looks out at the starry sky. He knows she's talking about Bianca. Finally he nods. Maybe he understands after all.

Reluctantly, he pulls on a life jacket.

"All right, let's go!" Aisha whispers, and turns the motor on.

CHAPTER 4

OUT ON THE WATER

Steering the boat out of the harbour feels magical under the starry sky. Aisha's never seen so many stars. It feels like they're there just for her.

Aisha wants to tell Sai that she thinks Bianca is up there watching out for her. But Aisha worries he'll say something stupid and ruin the moment. So, she doesn't say anything.

"Mum and Dad were really upset tonight," says Sai.

Aisha's hands clench the tiller. She really doesn't want to talk about this.

"So was I," she says. "I can't stand the way none of you will talk about her. It doesn't make any sense."

"Because it makes us all really sad," says Sai.

"It's worse not to talk about it," Aisha says. "And if this is why you came out here, you can just stop. I came out to get away from you guys."

Sai goes quiet. Aisha's glad about that. She's just starting to relax again when he points back at the harbour, which is getting further and further away.

"We should go back," Sai says nervously.

"Just a bit further," Aisha says. Every time she glances back and sees the harbour getting smaller, she breathes more easily.

Aisha takes a deep, deep breath. *There really is nothing better than sailing at night. Bianca would agree with me,* she thinks.

She turns off the motor and sets to work hoisting the sails. Sai helps her. They work in silence.

Aisha goes to the cockpit, grabs the halyard, and attaches it to the head of the mainsail, then raises the sail so it's expanded to catch the wind.

They make sure there isn't too much wind to use full sail. Next, they raise the jib using ropes and pulleys.

When both sails are hoisted, the wind catches them. They both watch the wind fill them up. The little boat comes alive. It moves eagerly over the water.

Aisha can tell even Sai is enjoying himself. He has a small hint of a smile on his face.

"You're smiling, Sai," Aisha teases. "I think this is your first one in months!"

Sai's small smile turns into a grin. He shakes his head at his sister.

The boat rocks gently underneath them. The stars get more and more brilliant the further away Aisha and Sai are from the lights of the harbour. The stars' reflection shines on the water.

Aisha closes her eyes for a while, letting the boat rock beneath her. She thinks of her sister.

Bianca loved the stars more than anything. She used to say she wanted to be an astronaut when she grew up – just so she could explore them.

CHAPTER 5

INCOMING STORM

"Whoa," says Sai.

Aisha opens her eyes and looks at Sai. He is pointing towards the sky, where thick, dark clouds are rolling in. The clouds are blotting out some of the brilliant stars. The wind picks up just a little bit.

"I've never seen clouds come in that fast," Sai remarks.

Aisha agrees. *It's kind of neat watching them roll in, though*, she thinks.

It's like they're alive too. The clouds come in so fast they remind her of a hungry pack of dogs.

Aisha's glad to be out on the water without Mum and Dad. They take any little change as a sign of danger.

But Sai has inherited their worry. "There's more and more of them," he says.

He's right. The clouds are now blotting out most of the stars. The wind picks up even more. It makes the waves around the boat choppier. The sails catch one of the big gusts of wind.

Sai keeps watching the waves. He has a worried look on his face. Another gust of wind fills the sails. The boat lurches a little. The waves rise.

"I don't like this," says Sai. "Let's go back. You said you only wanted to be out here for a minute anyway."

Aisha glances out over the water. The front of the boat bobs like a dolphin's nose through the swelling, restless water, up and down.

"We can make it before the storm. Don't worry," she says, but her voice doesn't sound very confident. They hear the first crack of thunder.

CHAPTER 6

STRANDED

"Turn the motor back on and get us back," Sai says.

He sounds stern and bossy again, the way he always does.

Aisha goes to turn on the motor. It roars for a few moments. Then, it sputters and dies.

"What's wrong with it?" says Sai. "It has enough gas, doesn't it?"

Aisha realizes she forgot to actually check how much fuel was in the tank before she left.

"No," she says in a small voice. "It must be out of fuel. It was only halfway full when I was out today."

"And you didn't check before you left?"
Sai's mad. His forehead crinkles.

Aisha doesn't have anything to say. She usually never makes mistakes like this. No one in their family does, not anymore. Dad always says a mistake on a boat can cost you your life. Bianca used to say that too. She always checked and double-checked everything, just like Dad.

Sai stands up but stumbles as a wave swells and the boat pitches.

For the first time, panic starts to fill Aisha. She can barely see the harbour from here – it's just tiny lights in the distance.

"The waves are just taking us further out," says Sai.

The wind grows stronger – now they can hear it rushing over the water and whipping at the sails. The waves grow higher. One of them sloshes over into the boat.

"Oh no," Aisha says.

Far out on the water, a bright strand of lightning rips through the sky. Thunder cracks somewhere near the shore.

A fat raindrop hits on Aisha's forehead.

"What should we do?" she asks. Her own voice comes out like a croak.

They've only been out on the boat during a storm once, and Dad and Bianca handled everything.

"I don't know," says Sai. "We don't want the wind taking us even further out."

"But without the sails, we won't have any power at all," she says. "We'll just be drifting."

Aisha feels another drop, and another. Another bolt of lightning tears through the sky. Now the clouds are thick and dark and right overhead. The harbour lights are barely specks.

They're not even in the bay anymore.

"We're in the ocean now," Aisha says, as the wind howls in the sails.

"Did you bring your phone?" Sai asks. He has to raise his voice so she can hear him.

Aisha shakes her head. "You?"

"No." He pats his pyjama bottoms. No pockets.

They stand there looking at each other, each trying to work this out.

Thunder crashes again. And then it's like the sky breaks open, and all the water in the world pours out.

CHAPTER 7

REEF THE SAILS!

The storm is fierce and sudden. They are both soaked in seconds. Aisha doesn't even have time to check if there's a spare poncho under the deck somewhere.

The waves are higher now than Sai or Aisha has ever experienced in the boat before. The boat pitches hard. Aisha holds herself steady. But Sai lurches and almost hits the bottom pole attached to the mainsail.

"What are we going to do?" Sai asks. He has to shout over the storm.

"I think we should reef the sails," she shouts back.

"What does that mean?" Sai asks.

"We need to set the sail so it's only part of the way up – enough so it'll still sail, but not so much that the strong winds overpower the boat and cause us to go off course," Aisha explains.

She doesn't know if this will work – or even if they can do it. She's never tried to reef the sails by herself. And she doesn't think Sai has either. Her dad has only ever talked her and Bianca through this once.

"We need to keep the boat going straight," Aisha says. She shouts directions at Sai, and they start reefing the sails.

"Careful!" Aisha says. "If the sail isn't properly reefed, the boat will weather helm and turn into the wind."

"But the wind is coming from the side of the boat now," Sai shouts back. "Do we need to change course?"

Aisha tries to position the tiller so the rudder will keep course as straight as possible.

If she and Sai try to sail across the big waves, they might even roll the boat if they don't manage the sails safely.

"We need to steer towards the flat spots!" Sai shouts.

Lightning streaks through the sky behind Sai. Aisha and Sai stumble around in the cockpit. But before they can do much of anything, the boat pitches – and then starts to roll onto its side.

CHAPTER 8

A TORN SAIL

Aisha screams and clings to one side of the boat. So does Sai. The wind tears against the sails.

If they capsize now, Aisha doesn't know if they'd be able to get back on the deck. Sai and Aisha look at each other.

"Throw your weight starboard!" she shouts.

With all their might, they run against the right side of the boat. They hope their weight will be enough to keep the boat upright.

For a few moments, the boat rocks at a dangerous angle. Water rushes in with a loud roar.

It sloshes everywhere. Aisha gets mouthfuls of sea and rainwater and can hardly see. It's hard to hold on to the side, since the rain has made everything so slippery.

They use all of their strength, but finally the boat rights itself again. It settles back onto the churning waves with a crash.

Aisha can barely stand up, her legs are so shaky. There's water in the bottom of the boat, and it's rising. Things from the boat are floating around Sai. He looks cold in his soaked pyjamas.

"Oh no!" Aisha gasps when she looks up at the sails.

The wind's blown out the headsail. The rip is long and bad. The fabric is flapping in the wind.

It's not good to have a torn sail still up. Aisha loosens the halyard, pulls the sail down and ties it up to secure it.

She stumbles back towards the mast to finish reefing the mainsail. With all the driving rain, it's hard for her to see what she's doing.

"Didn't you say we have to be on a steady course to reef the right way?" Sai asks.

"I don't know! I don't remember." She spits out some seawater and tries to think. She's shivering hard. More thunder cracks on the shore.

I've always helped Dad or Bianca with the sail, she thinks. *I know we can't risk another sail tearing. Without the motor, the sails are all we have.*

She decides to shorten the sail to the last reef point, leaving about thirty per cent up. She hopes it's the right thing to do. She's about to sit back in relief and exhaustion.

But Sai shouts, "Come on! We've got to pump this water out of here!"

CHAPTER 9

SEND A FLARE

The rain has let up a little, and now it's a light but steady rain. But there's still a load of water on the deck of the boat.

Aisha sloshes over to the bilge pump, near the tiller. She can use it to get rid of the water. Aisha grabs a little lever out of a cubbyhole and inserts it into the pump.

Sai and Aisha use the bilge pump like crazy to get the water out. There's at least a foot of it in the cockpit, and it's still raining. Their progress is slow.

"I think the rain's slowing down," Aisha says. But her voice sounds panicked.

They manage to get most of the water out. By the time they've finished, the rain has slowed to a drizzle.

They drop onto the seats of the cockpit, exhausted. Aisha's arms ache. Sai is shivering hard.

The waves are still choppy, and the clouds are still there. But the lightning and thunder seem further away.

Still, they can't see the harbour lights at all. They can't see anything except the night and the waves.

"Do we even know which direction is home anymore?" Aisha asks.

Sai doesn't answer at first. He looks around but only sees ocean. "No," he says finally.

"So even if we raise the full mainsail again, we won't know if we're headed in the right direction?" Her voice trembles.

Sai shakes his head. He looks miserable.

Aisha thinks about what this means. *If two kids are out here alone, with no motor and a torn sail, how will anyone find us?*

"There's got to be an emergency kit somewhere," she says.

"Good idea," says Sai.

They rummage in every corner of the boat they can think of. *Dad would know where it is. Bianca would too. She was always so good at remembering everything Dad taught us.*

Aisha's mad at herself for not paying better attention to where it's kept. But she never thought she'd be out on a boat without Bianca, either.

Finally, Sai finds an emergency kit. It was stashed in a compartment near the tiny pantry. There's no radio or walkie-talkie inside, but there are two things that could help: a little waterproof torch and a flare gun.

"Have you ever used one of these before?" Aisha asks Sai. He's holding it gently and aims it away from both of them, like he's worried it could fire unexpectedly.

"No, but we can work it out," he answers.

There's a little packet with instructions for the gun. Aisha turns on the torch and reads the instructions out loud to Sai.

He fires the flare gun into the air. It streaks bright into the black sky.

"It says to fire again in about ten minutes," she tells him.

"Yeah." He lowers the gun. "We shouldn't waste all our flares."

Aisha sits down again.

"So what now?" Aisha asks. She feels tiny, looking out at the endless blackness. A few pale stars peek through the clouds again. It's just enough to show them how lost they really are.

"I guess we wait." Sai sits down in his soaked pyjamas. He doesn't sound very hopeful either. "Hopefully someone notices us."

CHAPTER 10

SHE WANTS US TO REMEMBER

Neither Sai nor Aisha wears a watch, so they count the ten minutes until they send another flare. But Aisha loses track of counting as her thoughts start spinning out of control.

Aisha knows enough about the ocean to know the dangers. They could become dehydrated and die out here if no one finds them.

She can just imagine what Bianca would say to her.

"Bianca would never have got herself into a situation like this," Aisha says.

Sai winces. He looks like he wants to say something, but he just shrugs.

"I can't be like you guys, you know," Aisha blurts out. "Pretending Bianca never existed."

Sai frowns. "That's not what we're doing. There's just no point in talking about it."

"Yes, there is," she says. "To remember her. It's stupid not to talk about it."

He keeps frowning. "It's not like talking about her will bring her back."

"But don't you miss her?" she presses.

"Of course, I miss her!" Sai sounds more emotional than Aisha's ever heard him. "It's not about that."

"Then what is it about?" she shouts. Her voice sounds huge over the quietly lapping water.

Sai takes a big, long breath. Finally, he says, "I should have been able to save her."

Aisha is so surprised she just blinks at him. "Huh?"

"I should have been able to save Bianca. If I'd hung out with her that day, she wouldn't have got into the car with her friend. And she'd still be here."

She stares at him. She can't believe Sai thinks it was his fault.

"It wasn't your fault," Aisha says. "You didn't know that was going to happen. You had no idea."

Sai shrugs, but Aisha can tell he's trying not to cry. "It is my fault."

She goes over and sits next to him.

"No," she says. "She wanted to hang out with me that day too. And I was too busy with my school stuff." Aisha gives him a hug. "It's nobody's fault. She went off with her friends all the time. That was a normal thing for her to do."

Sai swallows and wipes his eyes.

"I should have been able to make it better for Mum and Dad," he says. "It's really hard seeing them go through this."

Aisha nods. "I know. I wish I could make it better for them too. But not talking about it isn't helping them or either of us. I know that for sure."

He sighs. "I don't know how we'll get Mum and Dad to talk about it."

"We'll make them." Aisha's heart swells up with hope. Maybe with Sai on her side, it will be easier. "We have to make a bold plan. The kind Bianca would have made. If we both refuse to eat until they talk about it, they'll have to give in."

Sai laughs. It's a sad laugh, but it's the first time in so long she's heard him laugh at all. "I really hope we won't have to starve ourselves."

Aisha looks out over the dark sea again. She can't explain it: even though she's scared for them, she feels like a big weight has been lifted off her chest.

"Do you think Bianca knows where we are?" she asks.

Sai looks up at the sky. "I don't know. But I know she would have wanted us to be happy."

"And that means talking about her and remembering her," she says.

Suddenly Sai leaps to his feet. "Hey – look!"

Aisha squints into the distance.

There, in the darkness, is another red flare.

CHAPTER 11

THE COAST GUARD

The flare flashes twice.

"It might be another boat," says Sai. "And they'll see our distress signal and call the Coast Guard."

They wait and wait. Then, eventually, they hear a much louder motor. And see big lights – a larger boat, moving towards them across the water.

A red light is on the right, green on the left, and a flashing blue light on top. It's the Coast Guard!

"We're saved!" Aisha cries out.

They both yell and jump up and down.

The motor gets louder and louder as the boat comes closer to them. The boat slows down as it approaches.

Someone shouts to Aisha and Sai, "Ten feet . . . five feet . . ." to let the pair know how close they are.

They do this until the boats are directly next to each other. Crew members quickly come out on deck and help Aisha and Sai clamber over onto their boat.

"Let's get you inside," one of them says. He leads Aisha and Sai to the cabin of the Coast Guard's boat.

"But what about our boat?" Aisha asks, looking back at it. "Mum and Dad will be so mad if it's left here."

"Don't worry. We're going to tow your boat," another crew member tells them. "We'll tie it on right now. You can watch from inside."

They drape thick blankets over the two kids. Sai and Aisha watch as the crew ties a tow line directly onto the eye bolt on the front of the sailing boat. It's the same bolt their dad uses to hitch the boat to the trailer.

"Line is attached!" someone calls.

The person driving the Coast Guard boat repeats, "Line is attached."

The engines roar back to life. The boat smoothly moves over the water, which is calm now.

The youngest crew member watches the sailing boat from the window.

"I'm on tow watch," he tells Aisha and Sai. "Just making sure your boat's OK back there."

It's so exciting slicing over the dark water, watching their boat cruise behind them. Aisha can almost forget what she's about to face. But she remembers as soon as the harbour lights come back into view.

The boat slows down as it approaches the harbour. Before they reach the docks, the coxswain calls, "Let me know when both boats are DIW."

Aisha knows DIW means "dead in the water", which is when boats have just stopped.

The Coast Guard boat reverses till it's right next to the sailing boat. Crew members start pulling the line back on board, and then climb onto the deck of the sailing boat to tie the two boats together. Once they're tied together side by side, they move forward again to the dock.

"Oh no," Aisha whispers.

It's almost dawn. The sky is turning blue-grey behind them. And there, standing on the dock, are their mum and dad.

CHAPTER 12

THE BIANCA

Aisha is very glad to see the dock. But she can also tell her parents are very upset. Mum has a blanket wrapped around her shoulders. There are police and an ambulance there. Several people from the neighbourhood are there too.

"I bet that ambulance is there to take us to hospital," Sai says. "To make sure we're OK."

Aisha nods. She feels like she's gone mute. She can't believe that this whole time, she didn't think about the trouble she'd be in when she got home. It all hits her now.

She starts sweating. *My parents will never let*

me sail again, she thinks. *They'll never let me do anything again. I'll be grounded for life.*

At least they didn't completely wreck the family boat. She hopes that will make her parents a bit less angry.

One of the family's friends helps the Coast Guard crew tie the sailing boat to the dock, and then the crew works on freeing their boat from the sailing boat. Meanwhile, Aisha and Sai step off the boat.

Their parents rush up and hug them so hard Aisha feels like she might pop.

"What were you thinking?" Mum cries out before Aisha or Sai could greet them.

Their mum doesn't wait for a response but continues to yell for about five minutes. Dad stands there silent, wiping his eyes. Even though he's crying, Aisha can tell he's furious too.

While Aisha's mum is yelling, the police

and ambulance people check to make sure Aisha and Sai don't have any serious injuries. Then they head over to talk to the Coast Guard.

"The police are going to want to talk to you," Dad says. "They can't believe you'd do something like this, either."

"I know taking the boat out without telling you was wrong. And I'm really sorry." Aisha grabs Sai's hand. "But it's not OK to not talk about Bianca anymore. I can't stand it. I can't stand being at home, knowing we're not even allowed to talk about her."

Mum and Dad look at each other. Their faces are surprised and sad.

"We wondered if that had anything to do with this," Dad said.

Aisha tenses up, waiting for him to yell.

Instead, he surprises her.

He looks uncomfortable as he kneels down.

"I'm sorry, kids," their dad says. "When you were gone, Mum and I were so scared we were going to lose you too. We realized . . ." He scratches his head. "We realized we haven't been dealing with Bianca's death in a way that's helpful to you."

Aisha can't believe her ears. She looks at Sai to see if he's hearing it too. Even he looks amazed.

"So . . . we can talk about her?" Aisha asks. "I don't do it to make you sad. It's because I miss her."

Aisha and Sai's parents smile. Both of them are crying.

"It will be hard," Mum says. "But we'll be more open about it. We can't run away from our feelings forever."

Sai clears his throat. "It does feel better to talk about it."

The ambulance people come over. "Are

you kids ready? We want to take you up to the hospital to look you over."

Aisha hugs her parents again, and then hugs Sai too.

She glances back at their little boat. Her heart swells up. The boat got them safely through the storm.

"Before we go," Aisha says, "I thought of the perfect name for our boat. *The Bianca.*"

AUTHOR BIO

Salima Alikhan has been a freelance writer and illustrator for fourteen years. She lives in Texas, USA, where she writes and illustrates children's books. One of her projects, *Emmi in the City: A Great Chicago Fire Survival Story*, was published in 2019 as part of Capstone's Girls Survive series. Salima also teaches creative writing at St. Edward's University and English at Austin Community College.

ILLUSTRATOR BIO

Eva Morales is a professional Spanish 2D artist and illustrator living near the Mediterranean Sea. She has worked in children's publishing, TV, film production and advertising for about fourteen years. Now she works as a full-time freelance illustrator, using a combination of digital and traditional techniques. Eva loves to walk on the beach and read books in her spare time.

GLOSSARY

bilge pump water pump used to remove extra water from a boat

boom horizontal pole on a boat that helps control the sail

cockpit part of a boat where the controls are located

halyard rope used for raising or lowering the sail

hoist raising or lifting the sails

jib another word for the smaller headsail in front of the mast

knots abbreviation for the way sailors measure boat speed, in nautical miles per hour

mainsail sail rigged on the mainmast of a boat

reef roll up or fold part of a sail

starboard right side of the boat when facing the same direction as the boat

tiller bar attached to a boat's rudder, used for steering

weather helm tendency of a sailing boat to go into the wind

DISCUSSION QUESTIONS

1. Why was Aisha so upset at the beginning of the story? What could she have done differently to communicate her feelings to her family?

2. Sai had a different reaction to missing Bianca. In what ways is Sai's personality different from Aisha's? Give examples from the story to support your answer.

3. Why do you think the boat was one of Aisha's favourite places to be?

WRITING PROMPTS

1. The sea is a very special place to Aisha. Is there a place in nature that's very special for you? Write about it.

2. Aisha wishes her family would talk about her sister's death. Was there ever a time when you wished people would share their feelings? Write about it. Compare your experience to Aisha's.

3. Aisha forgot to make sure the boat's motor had enough fuel, but she and Sai managed to stay safe and get help. Talk about a time that you forgot to do something important. How did you handle it?

MORE ABOUT SAILING

Sailing is a fun and popular sport. It's also a great way to get places that big ships full of tourists can't go. Sailing boats can dock on small hidden islands that bigger craft can't get to.

The youngest person to circumnavigate the world solo is a Dutch sailor called Laura Dekker. "Circumnavigate" means going around, or circling, the whole world.

Dekker started her journey in 2012. When she passed through French Polynesia, she followed the same route her parents had taken twenty years earlier.

Almost two years and 43,450 kilometres (27,000 miles) later, Dekker completed her trip. She was 16 years old. Her experience was documented in the 2014 film *Maidentrip*. Dekker also wrote a book about her record-breaking trip called *One Girl One Dream*.

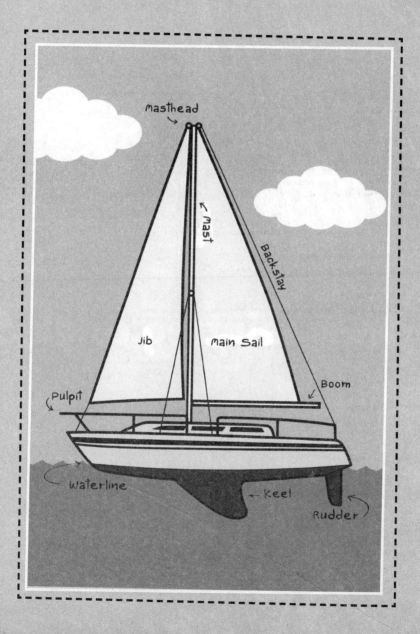